That What Lies Below

Octavius Anglicus

Published by Octavius Anglicus, 2023.

THAT WHAT LIES BELOW

First edition. February 18, 2023.

ISBN: 979-8215300084

Written by Octavius Anglicus.

Table of Contents

THAT WHAT LIES BELOW.................................... 1

THE THING WITHIN 25

HERMES..29

THRONEIS 37

VOID..41

CLOSE..43

This book is adressed to one Howard Phillips Lovecraft,
for showing me the door,

In memoriam of Kallie, for always insisting herself a
lady-like lap-dog, in spite of her endless drooling and
great size saying otherwise,

And acknowledgements are made to friends, for their
efforts in pushing my writing to be the best it can, and
the assurance I ever could.

The oldest and strongest emotion of mankind is fear, and the oldest and strongest kind of fear is fear of the unknown.

HPL: Supernatural Horror in Literature

THE AUTHOR

Writer of weird.

Find more at:
https://octaviusanglicus.wordpress.com/

FOREWORD

I have often referred to Octavius Anglicus as a Renaissance man: from his study of language to his literary knowledge, to his more mundane interests ranging from music composition to athleticism, but nowhere is this title more aptly applied than to his writing. Octavius expertly fuses science fiction and horror with Lovecraftian elements that produce a fascinating and straightforward piece of weird fiction. In these pages you will find tales of madness, long forgotten fertility cults, the forbidden knowledge that comes from exploring the cosmos, the impending dread of what lurks behind closed doors, and much more. I hope, dear readers, you enjoy this work of surreal speculative fiction as much as I have.

Amber Espindola, 3rd February 2023

PREFACE

As though another entity had used my internal voice to whisper the idea to me, on the twelfth of February, 2022, I heard the phrase *'that what lies below'* softly pass through my mind; my initial instinct was to contact a close friend, Amber Espindola, and ask her thoughts on this phrase for the title of a horror story, and, with her approval, I would spare no time in creating a story for said title, a story that I would, by July of the same year, realise I had been stretching in order to fit the length of a standard novel at the price of its quality, concluding I should instead write That What Lies Below however long or short it need be, and write other short stories to go with it; and so this book became an anthology.

By August, the story idea I originally had planned for the title *That What Lies Below* I grew unloving of, and opted in the end to begin a new story—the one found in this very book. In the same month, three other short stories would also begin to develop, the first of which being *Hermes*, a story that I came up with when reminded that other apes and monkeys have before been sent to outer space in place of human astronauts, and so I put together a story of a chimpanzee encountering a horror on such a venture to the above. The other story, *Close*, I unravelled in my head as was walking my dog in order to be away from home for some moments after receiving a fright, a walk on which I would see, but, unfortunately, due to the species generally disliking my dog, not be able to greet a black and white cat I have been acquainted for some time now who reminds me fondly of Pat's Jess, which did calm me. Anyhow, the reason for my alarm is that as I was getting out of the shower, the bathroom door opened, so I closed it, yet it opened again, and so I would close it again; now, on the third time the door opened, and I could have sworn I saw the door handle moving down and up again, and I froze for some seconds before opening the door to check and confirm that no one, not a thing, was on the other side, and it was so, so I closed the door. A fourth time the door opened, and I kicked it shut in alarm. I had to work up some will to open that door, and when I did so, after inspecting the house in its entirety, I did not wish to be inside of it for just a little while. There are two pronunciations to the spelling *c-l-o-s-e*; if asked which is the correct for its usage as the title of the final short story in this book, I can only repeat that there are indeed two pronunciations for the spelling *c-l-o-s-e*.

As for the third story, *Egg*, it was renamed *Ei* and removed from this book as it no longer fit in, but will return to be published another time. In October, the story *The Thing Within* was created after a re-read of HPL's *The Beast in the Cave*; one line in particular stood out to me, which would serve as *The Thing Within*'s epigraph; an emotion struck me that I wished to emulate in writing.

By the end of January 2023, I had full drafts of all five short stories one can read in this book, *Throneis* being written as the fifth story on the twenty-eighth of January in no more than twenty minutes, an idea conjured as I was having a dark hot chocolate and a slice of Victoria sponge cake at a small café which always makes me wish my literary friends did not live so afar so we could meet up in said café on a monthly basis to discuss and critique one another's writings.

On the first of February, I sent an up-to-date draft of this book, the *introduction* and *preface* as-of-yet unwritten, to the afore-mentioned Amber Espindola for her to read as she had agreed to write a foreword, and as I did, a closed door opened by itself. I sent the draft also to some other friends, and continued a cycle of proof-reading and editing I had began ... I'm not sure when, I didn't write it down.

That very night I had a strange dream: a man flung off a ferry to be eaten by sharks, but the water is untrue, and a basement of human cadavers hung from hooks, their heads replaced with those of pigs. That's the gist of what I saw.

Two days later, the third of February, I am sent the foreword for this book, and immediately a door opens by itself. A guest arrives shortly after to pass through the very same door.

Now I lie in bed in the early hours of the fourth of February, 2023, having written the *introduction*, currently writing the *preface*, and come daylight I will proof-read and edit this book one final time, and then it will be published. I am not sure why I wait until the daylight hours, perhaps it is merely a habit, I have no ability to sleep this night, and there is something strange about the sky; it is not black and there are no stars; it is all a dull grey, and I know this isn't just a big cloud because I can see the true clouds moving. It is 03:44. The sky is incorrect.

INTRODUCTION

That What Lies Below is birthed from a place of love for the works of H.P. Lovecraft (HPL), whom the world of horror literature are greatly indebted to. One of the three names seen as the triumvirate of the golden age of weird fiction, HPL crafted many tales to reflect the idea that the most primal and greatest fear is that of the unknown; and it is my belief that not only was he a master of his craft, but few others have come close to his greatness. And yet, while his writings are now rightfully recognised by many for their creative and linguistic genius, with finding any modern horror writer—or even writers of other genres such as low fantasy—not influenced by his works a tremendous challenge, they would never be so until many years after HPL's death in 1937, aged forty-six.

One of the greatest travesties and tragedies of horror literature remains to be HPL not only never knowing how great of an impact he would have on the genre, potentially more influential than any other— including this very book, with all short stories here taking direct influence from HPL—, but he believed himself to be quite the opposite, a small, unimportant name who would likely be forgotten.

I, and the literary world of horror as a whole for that matter, owe HPL a greater deal than any one of us could ever hope to pay back; and so it is only fitting my first book under this penname for weird fiction be dedicated to his name.

THAT WHAT LIES BELOW

That is not dead which can eternal lie,
And with strange aeons even death may die.

HPL: The Nameless City

OCTAVIUS ANGLICUS

I. Voyage Unto the Unknown

There is no need for me to re-establish what is already known of the BM-AMNH archaeological expedition I was a part of in the Summer of 2019; I am sure you have read the various newspapers, or seen on the television, all there is to know of what has been told. What I shall detail, however, are the events that transpired aboard, and post-sinkage, of Emma, of which we all agreed upon never speaking of; an agreement we all came to without the need to utter any words of discussion.

Of course, dear reader, you know that there were seven from the British Museum, and seven from the American Museum of Natural History, and you may find information regarding the ship's crew and the physical dimensions of the ship and many more details if need be, but what you will not know of is that there was an extra passenger who snuck himself aboard the ship, us all none the wiser until he revealed himself only some days prior to the sinkage. This rather-welcomed intruder was blacker than the night, save for his green eyes that would stare into our own in curiosity, shadowed by the affectionately blinking he gave us all, and those white fangs he would reveal in his meowing for attention—or when he hissed, not at any of us in particular, but the ocean he seemed to loathe. This black tomcat we all grew to love, and even, strangest of all, Thomas would pet him, and his otherwise severe allergy would never react to this particular cat. During the trip, several names had been suggested for him, but in the end we settled upon an amalgamation of two of these names: Black Tom, from the name Blackie—I do not quite remember who came up with this one, though the meaning behind it seems clear enough—, and Thomas, not named after the strangely no-longer allergic Thomas, but suggested by Hayes as 'male cats are tomcats'—a respectable man he was, but even he suffered the same curse of uncreativity standard of an American.

Anyhow, this Black Tom would wander the ship freely, coming out of the shadows to any one of us for attention whenever he yearned for it, and was particularly fond of laying upon his back for his belly to be rubbed, only to—albeit playfully—scratch the arms of he who took the bait, his green eyes leering at the unsuspecting victim's hands as they approached. It was on the night of Emma's sinkage he came to my cabin—which I had been sharing with three others also from the British Museum, but they were elsewhere—, and jumped up on the desk I was leant over, viewing my work, the work of us all, ancient texts with a newly discovered ancient language, the very reason we were headed out to sea in the first place, in hope to find that island we all said we hadn't. In looking over my notes, Black Tom found one symbol of particular interest; this symbol I appeared to most likely be the island's name, but the etymology was a strange one, deriving from the verbs 'to lie' and 'to trap' (the latter of which comes from the noun meaning 'fence' or 'wall,' thus being to 'fence-' or 'wall-in'), the adverb 'below,' and the pronoun 'it,' this symbol can be translated '[where] it lies entrapped below.' A strange name to be sure, I had not many ideas what this imprisoned figure could be, the references to this island far and few between, the writers giving few words on it, those words all negative.

To something only he could hear, the tomcat hissed suddenly, sending vague threats in every which way. I asked what was the matter with him, and he responded with a sympathetic meowing, staring those eyes of his directly into my own; the dark green of those irides seemed a green alien to this world in those moments, and my mind flickered through all the lexicon I knew until my own internal voice was used by another: 'lifeboat,' it said.

A perplexed pause on my part.

Then something rammed the ship from below, causing a violent side-to-side rocking.

'Lifeboat,' the other said with my internal voice again. This time I acted on the warning, pocketting my penknife from the desk and taking Black Tom into my arms, and headed for the stairs, being thrown to and thro every step of the way. A sudden rushing of water emerged coming from the top of the steps just as I had reached, then a just-as-sudden springing of myself upward, smashing into the ceiling; I, somewhat hazed, would switch to holding Black Tom in one arm, the other clutching tightly to the railing; these springings and side-to-side rockings continued as I went up the stairs, as did the rushings of water down them; but I did, against all odds, make it atop to the deck.

There I saw ... that thing, or a part of it, lit up by the twitching lights of Emma, wrapping about her with its grabbers all along the her sides, trying to pull her down, the waters on the ocean rushing into her as she was held downward into water, just enough for the ocean's water to spill onto the deck as it rocked; but, perhaps to toy with its prey, its grip loosened, and a great thud came from below, launching Emma, along with myself, and Black Tom, and anyone else still aboard her, into the air, before we came crashing back down. I was unscathed from this crashing down, however, in getting to my feet, I slipped upon the wet deck, and the back of my head collided with something hard.

Everything became a blur then, and I can only remember the next order of events in-between intervals of this blurred consciousness.

I remember a black fluff standing atop my chest, staring at me, its head momentarily leaning to one side, before it darted off elsewhere. My eyes closed and all I could feel was dizziness, being otherwise devoid of any feeling whatsoever.

In the next interval, someone was carrying me atop his shoulder, and not-so-gently—though unintentionally—dropped me into what I can now conclude was the lifeboat. Though I could not see any face clearly, my rescuer must have been Hayes, whom I had befriended during the journey with him teaching me poker, and I teaching him cribbage, as he was the only black face among us. Immediately, another two were attending to my head, holding it steady as we dropped into the ocean, and, if I'm to guess, attempting to stop the bleeding, I'm not sure, my consciousness faded away once again just as we hit the water, my head once again thudding against a hard surface.

The black fluff was sat atop my chest again, flinching away from any water splashing onto the lifeboat. One of the Americans had managed to bring his rifle, using it to shoot things in the water, clubbing them away with the buttstock when they tried to climb aboard, the others making do to fight with their fists, or, perhaps, it is possible they were able to find some small items to use as weaponry, it's hard to tell. In the midst of this chaos, something grabbed me, more of its kind grabbing some others, too, pulling us into the depths. The black fluff jumped after me, and those humanoid shapes let go of us to face the cat. In my blinks, I saw the cat disappear, and something else take its place; some of the humanoid sea-creatures continued charging, others fled. Whatever happened next, I am uncertain of the details, as I faded away from consciousness, assuming this would be my end, as gravity dragged me down to the depths of the abyss.

THAT WHAT LIES BELOW

II. As Above

Upon a sand-beach I lay as I awoke, hazed and tired; each and every movement I made sent a shot of pain across my skull. There was no regurgitating of water—perhaps I had done it as a came ashore, either in my unconscious state or for a brief moment of consciousness I have forgotten. I took my time turning to my right—not that I had much choice in the matter, my left arm shaking dramatically, weak and limp—in turning myself from being face-down to face-up, feeling the closed penknife in my pocket press against my thigh as I did so, and, arching my legs, lifted my torso so I would be in a seated positing. My vision was not as blurred anymore, but still somewhat so, and I found the brightness of the Sun too much of an irritant to be able to look moreso toward it than away, them shivering whenever I did so, and found myself taking many slow and hard blinks. Looking at the sand I saw the markings my unconscious body had left; as I recall, it looked less like I had been washed ashore, and more so I had been dragged. Making the logical conclusion someone else would have had to drag me, I called out hoarsely and meekly, but no answer came.

In trying to stand, I initially succeeded, but fell to my knees shortly afterwards, the sudden movement causing an equally sudden shooting pain throughout my mind, and, leaning over onto my knees and one good hand, regurgitated a small amount of what I had last ate—porridge, if I'm not mistaken. Raising my head slightly, I saw the island we were truly headed for; what I found myself upon was an oval-shaped sand-hill, the peak protruding just slightly from the water, perhaps fifteen feet across the longer diameter, and ten feet the shorter. And on the other island, its shore perhaps only forty feet from the shore of mine, I could just make out a lifeboat that, judging by its positioning, looked as though it had not been beached, but, like me, dragged from the waters. That, I knew, would be where the others were, if any were left.

I could not stand, but I could crawl into the water, a crawl that quickly morphed to a gentle swim. What I was not expecting as I looked down on occasion was a strange net made from what I can only describe as things of the sea running betwixt the two islands; a queer thing to be sure, but what truly frightened me was the shark I saw trapped within it. My initial reaction panicked me to a frenzied splash as I had not realised it was trapped, but when I did, I realised I could kill it—of course, this thought was an incorrect one as the penknife I had with me did not have a long enough blade to both pierce the skin and hit the brain, but one must remember in reading this my mind was hazed and I illogically assumed this fish to have, in spite of its lack of hands, been what grabbed and pulled me from the lifeboat earlier. So I swam the odd foot or so downward to reach the net, then climbed it down another two or three so as to reach the shark, and pulled out and opened my blade to strike it ... but I could not. The fish wasn't even trying to bite me, she—I would be told later on she was female—only tried constantly to swim out of her entrapment with no success. So I took my penknife, and gradually sawed away at the strange ropes of this net, which could handle a great force of pulling but were cut through with surprising ease, going back up for air whenever need be, keeping my travels up and down steady as to avoid further striking pains across my mind, and soon she was free. She swam around me, investigating her saviour with those black eyes; in any other case I would have been frightened by a circling shark, but somehow I knew she meant no harm, only to act on her curiosity, before disappearing into the murky depths. I reascended and kept my swimming slow, cautious of whatever could have trapped that shark, my limbs always under the water to avoid splashing if it hunted via detecting vibrations in the water just as sharks do, and in short time found myself crawling up the shore of the greater island. I rolled onto my back, closed my eyes, and drifted off to a sleep.

My awakening was not a natural one; rather, my internal voice, again controlled by another, awoke me; its exact words are not of importance, but they were spoken so loudly and so suddenly I sprang erect before even realising I had done so; upon my realisation came a spell of dizziness so great that I fell back from my weightless legs to a sitting. The aching, while still an at the present problem, I found to be much more tolerable, and my eyesight had almost fully returned, the eyes themselves no longer shivering in response to looking more toward the sun than away from it; my left arm still shook quite noticeably. Not being too rested, but just enough so as to enough to function; I reckon I had taken a short nap, perhaps fifteen minutes. I rose to my feet again, this time slowly, and was relieved to find myself finally being able to find a balance, if just barely, and looked around for any sign of the others.

I found one other by sight, not any one person, but the black tomcat, sitting elegantly where the forest—or what resembled one—met the beach, looking directly at me, as if patiently awaiting my coming. As I took my first awkward step towards him, he immediately darted off into those strange trees, the strangeness of which I could at that time only feel being there, yet to notice the cause of why I felt that way of them. Other than the lack of leaves, they seemed ordinary, almost like oak trees, only thinner.

My awkward steps continued, until I myself was the borderline of these two biomes, where my connection to the world changed so greatly I stood there for several minutes before taking any more steps, having to muster great will-power to force myself to, something within cautioning this area was for no thing of Earth to step into; it was not alive, but nor was it dead, it simply was.

For some time I kept walking true to what I thought a straight line, anxiously turning suddenly at random intervals; did something watch? Did something whisper just then? Did those things that attacked us in the waters have legs, and follow us onto land? There was naught and aught all across the eldritch forest, and I was afraid. I found myself tripping over one root that went in a pattern of many bows from the tree it (presumably) came from, each bow half the size of the last, and I began to run as those voices of slience screamed their whispers; I tripped upon a similar string of bowed roots, coming up fast to continue my sprint, my vision worsening as I did, a fire exploding from the depths of Hell from my mind and across my whole body; another similar root I tripped over, before begin my sprint again; the eyes watched but they were not there; and another root; and another sprint; I stepped over yet another, only knowing I had when the second foot kicked against it, knocking me over, and it was here I realised this was the same root; my straight path had impossibly curved. Those whispers of silence suddenly died away; the invisible eyes closed; I calmed, though still retained some anxiety.

Not to worry about getting lost, seeing how easily one could in on this accursed island, I realised I could simply mark the tress as I went; so I pulled out my penknife, and as I pressed the blade into the nearest tree, that was when I noticed what was so strange about them: they weren't trees at all, at least not any kind that should be. They looked like trees,having branches coming from the main body, which themselves had further branches, which could then branch off again, and so on, but I did not feel wood against the palm I had rested against the tree as I pressed my blade against it with the other, I felt air, air so compressed it could be rested on; as my hand and the knife slowly sunk into the tree, I knew it was fluid in nature. My hand I pulled out from the tree before I could be sucked in wholly, but my knife I had lost. Whatever membrane had kept the gaseous tree together tore where I pulled out my hand, and from it bled droplet by droplet the dark gas within, each droplet driving itself slowly through the air in the same direction. I followed this path of droplets in their curving and zigzagging and sudden hard turns, true straightness in this meeting-point of two worlds.

I was so warm and drowsy walking this path laid out by those black droplets.

Eventually I heard familiar voices where the droplets headed, and went toward them, picking up my pace. I called out as I approached and they turned to see my arriving. My head grew warm and heavy, and ached; the rest of me losing its weight. My eyes closed just as I was falling down.

Coming to, I found myself under the orange light of dawn, having apparently slept through the dusk and night, where I lay aside a stream deep into the forest, the water rushing quickly and loadly. On sighting this stream were any hopes I had of prior events being a dream extinguished, as it was a ring, with no rivers branching from it, nor any waterfalls flowing into it, yet the water danced chaotically, as if spinning both ways at once, the waves violently clashing with one another; and from another side of the ring, I saw a queue of gaseous droplets floating in the air, heading toward the ring, heading into the chaotic dance of water, uninflicted by it, as though they were trasversing two different planes of existence. In the centre of the ring stood a pyramid, though I would say its shape was more conical.

I took notice that my left arm still shook; I should tell you bluntly, dear reader, as you may have already concluded, that arm still shakes somewhat to this day.

The others noticed I had awoke and saw to me. Twelve of us were there in total (including myself); four of the Americans, four of the British, four of the ship's crew (which had, in fact, been Americans). One of the other eleven was Jack Hayes, who revealed it was he who rescued me from going down with Emma, and told me that Timothy, who had been attending to my injured self on the lifeboat, along with George, the American who had brought his rifle to the lifeboat, did not make it, lost to the sea, or rather the things that lurked within it. He also told me whoever had still been aboard Emma after us was surely dead, as he saw the limbs of the great thing tighten, breaking her apart in its grip, dragging her down; his face and voice became empty as he described those screams from Emma, and the silencing of them as she was pulled below.

A pause.

'It was the cat that told me you needed help,' Hayes said suddenly, breaking the melancholic silence; 'it came to me and, in spite of the noise of the wind and the rain and the waves, gave a meow loud enough to hear, and looked from me to where you lay. But the funny thing is, when I hesitated, as I couldn't tell what you were at that distance in those conditions, I had a strange feeling of something looking for the right word within my mind, and then my voice—my voice in my head that is—said your name, and I knew then it was you I saw. But that voice, it was mine yet not me who spoke with it.' I shared in response my experience with the same thing right before the ship began to sink, both of us noting the cat was present in both circumstances, but neither fully grasping the importance of that fact yet.

There had been debate about what way to go as I was unconscious, he added, but in the end they settled on what I had: to follow the gas, carrying me along the journey. Now with me being awake, we were ready as a group to enter the pyramid.

Getting over the stream was of no difficulty, no more than a foot wide, though each of us took some seconds of hesitation before leaping. I went second-to-last, almost slipping back as my landing caused a spell of dizziness to strike me, having to grabbed by three on the front, and Hayes, the last to jump, on the back, pushed and pulled to be upright again. All of us could confirm one would feel steam going over that warfare of white waters, just as one would if holding a bare hand above a saucepan of boiling water.

Upon entry, our duty to the sciences took hold as we focused our concern to only the primitive paintings on the walls, and they told the story of it all, of the island's creation, of the thing below it, and of three particular cats, two white, each aside a black one. I saw the paintings tell a tale of how these three cosmic cats used the people they had discovered to cross the seas, where they would conjure and island to entrap a cosmic power they feared. The cats had to show their true forms to face the cosmic horror, not knowing these impossible shapes would drive their people to madness; those who caught sight of the cats' true forms fled to the sea, carcinising and growing more fish-like, and those that saw what cosmic entity the cats feared simply died. Something else struck me about the paintings, a map of the world, which unmistakably showed Pangaea, a map of the world drawn almost two million years before the Homo sapien appeared. These people the cats had been benevolent to and worshipped by were ancient, far more ancient than any simian; through similar niches, two species evolved converging towards the same result.

I was never studying a human language.

THAT WHAT LIES BELOW

The dance of the paintings came to an end, our sights focusing back to reality, and we all turned to the same entrance where Black Tom stood with a sad look on his face. He leaned his front end down in a stretch and yawned before gracefully lowering himself to a sitting. He pointed his green eyes to the centre of the stone flooring where a tablet of gold lay in a perfectly-sized gap, engraved with the same ancient language of those false-simians I had been studying. I picked up the tablet and inspected the words; I do not know how these words would be pronounced, the language and its people long extinct, but I could work out an approximate translation within my mind, and as I did so, the mere thought of these ritual prayers caused the ring of water to shoot suddenly out and surround the pyramid wholly, lowered so as to place the structure in whole below the ground, as it dragged us in circles, then suddenly we were slung, not across any physical distance, but across planes of existence; all, save the cat, who lay calmly upon the tablet I had dropped in my panic, clung to a side, somehow all feeling as if we were being thrown to what side we had leant against, screaming silently in the noiseless place between worlds. A sudden halt came to the pyramid, and the water began to gently lower itself to a ring again. Ourselves no longer pinned against the inner-walling. We found ourselves in an other place than before. We fell down.

III. So Below

I believe we had all fallen comatose, until the cat, not troubled by the crossing of planes whatsoever, forcefully awoke us, intruding our minds with its own to fix whatever had been broken upon our arrival.

Coming to, we were reinvigorated, taking no time to transition from where we lay to standing without the pyramid. So energised were we, in fact, that it took until we were without the pyramid to notice that all of our movements were trailing, for lack of a better term; for instance, when I moved my hand before my eyes, each area of space it had occupied left a momentary imprint, so I could see each instance of where it was in space; each imprint was separated by time-gaps so small the naked eye could not possibly tell how many were being imprinted every second, but we could count that it took seven-to-eight seconds for an imprint to fully fade away (that is, at least, to the naked eye, of course). Yes, we all trailed, with the exception of—as all oddities from our supposed side of whatever inter-cosmic conflict we had stumbled upon favoured—Black Tom.

In seeing him stride gracefully uninflicted by the natural laws of this plane, I was forced to accept yet another impossibility: he was a power from beyond this plane, far beyond our own, too, but has walked said two planes, as well as his own, and perhaps many more, far longer than our species has walked upright; he was the black cat from primitive paintings of the pyramid.

Just as before, there was the same ring of violently thrashing rapids surrounding the pyramid, its waves trailing just as we did,

THAT WHAT LIES BELOW

but it did not run across a trench of any sort, for there was no ground of any sort running across the out rim of the river-ring, and what other lands could be sighted, too, were disconnected, gaps between them leading to a great void. Looking up, I saw how this world operated; this world's star was in the centre of it, but that star was also Its prison; just like Earth, this world was spherical, only we were on the inside of the sphere, hollowed out, landmasses split not by oceans and rivers but blackness, tears in the fabric of the plane, where things could slip through to our own, thus the strange gaseous trees on that island when bleeding had simply returned to their native habitat through the closest tear they could find, the river-ring. This was not a full plane, if such terminology will suffice, as ours is, but a pocket-plane of a sort, shaped within our own, ours warped ever so slightly to compensate for it. Allow me to elaborate: imagine, if you will, you have a milkshake in a cup, and use a straw to drink; now, I'm sure many of us, especially so as children, have blown into the straw rather than sucked; when one blows, bubbles will appear, and the milkshake is warped by these bubbles to compensate for their existence. Our cosmos is the milkshake, and this inverted world is a bubble created by the black cat and those two white cats that were with him many aeons ago.

We had to sprint to gain the speed necessary to clear the rushing waters and the gap that followed all in one, landing on the next island, jumping in the same order as we had above, surprisingly with less struggle; gravity seemed a little, though not greatly, weaker within this plane. The cat leapt over following our leaps, no run-up needed for him to do so. On this island, on all the islands of this inverse-planet, there were those trees of thick black gas, among other flora, likewise akin to our own but bastardised to be unnatural things.

We walked through the accursed façade of a forest, taking care to watch our step in paranoia of our every surrounding. The first fauna we saw came to us in great swarms; quadrapedal slugs, their limbs to small to be of any use, with wings that were far greater than their bodies, as one may observe a bird's typically are; it was just as slimy as its sluggish appearence would have suggested, a pinky-white colour, throwing droplets of this stringy yellow substance with each flap of the wings that flapped quickly and buzzed loudly alike a dragonfly. Lacking any real threat, they were otherwise a nuisance, constantly landing themselves upon us to slither across, fluttering in by our faces to dart sparodically hither and thither as a fly would; and so we began to clutch and rip and tear the slug-things in rage, throwing them against the ground and squashing them under our shoes, beating them with our fists, ourselves drenched in their slime and brown goo I would guess to be their blood and entrails; even Black Tom joined in our rage, slicing many apart with his claws, claws that left marks bigger and deeper than should have been possible from his claws.

No matter our efforts, long-lasted as they were, the slug-troopers would be reinforced, and it was hard to fight with the trailing making a difficulty of keeping track of our own selves, so we stopped our onslaught and instead killed only as they came to us, and continued our walking.

THAT WHAT LIES BELOW

Only some moments later, we found the next fauna, or rather it had found us: a queen, who was just a great rolling body with four arms and a face on her stomach, and her four smaller males guarding her; the five snacked on enclosing slugs as casually as a horse licks flies off its own eyes, eyeing us greedily; where we flinched in fear, Black Tom, pounced to stand between us and the beasts. Dancing between the four guards' attacks, he took many beatings, but still came out the victor, if just barely, and now faced the Queen. The two charged; the Queen caught Tom in her grip and swung him about when he attempted clawing his way up her limb, now clawing in a feeble attempt to escape her grasp. He scratched out her eyes that encircled her mouth as she tried to eat him; but strangely, I swear by it, his claws had never reached her eyes. She slammed him down in a fit of rage, the two combatants both gravely injured, who would prevail as victorious uncertain to anyone.

I do not know who was the first to charge, but whoever it was did, and one-by-one we all followed suit, ripping the great beast apart with our bare hands, tearing the flesh away from bone, until blood and organs drenched us. Nothing remained of the queen. I remember laughing for just a few moments. I believe the othes also laughed. Killing that thing was perhaps the greatest relief any of us had ever felt in our lives.

The cat had fallen to his side, too injured to walk on; I took the role of his carrier.

He continued to guide us on our way, the slug menaces bothering us still. Our wrath was still unleashed upon these pests as we went our way, though, exhausted mentally and physically from our slaying of the great beast, we were more conservative with our extermination. Soon enough, we reached our destination: a stone circular table, exactly the size needed for twelve to stand comfortably around it with a foot between each individual.

Upon the stone table I laid Black Tom, and he meekly crawled to the centre as we all took our positions around the circular body, uniting our hands, and let our tongues be controlled by his will. What alien language came out I am uncertain if I am able to even begin to describe, his tongue spoken with ours, and all the trees collapsed, the gases of many colours rushing over to the table, spinning quickly like a hurricane perfectly in line with the rim of the table, blinding us wholly from black Tom, until the gases united as a smoke of—pink? Purple? It was not a colour that ought to be—, clouding our view only partially now, blurring the image of Black Tom, now raised up—down?—into the air, only now he was no cat, but his true self, our sanities saved only due to the smoke-hurricane partially blocking us from a full-viewing. A kaleidoscopic madness of black shadows battling for one another's spaces, rings of white fangs spinning alike saw-blades as they flung themselves all over, and those endless green eyes what opened in one placed, dissappeared to the blackness as they closed, and reappeared elsewhere as they opened; this image seemed two-dimensional, but whether that was his form following its own rules or the smoke giving an effect similar to that of how a fish-tank makes the fish within look flat I cannot say. The black shadows reached out, and shot out to engulf the star in the centre of this world, imploding the star to a black hole; we were pulled towards it, still hand-in-hand, still chanting, and then ...

Nothing. There is nothing for me to say here to provide any explanation of our return to our reality; one second we were being dragged to a black hole within the other place, the next we all awoke together in a circular pattern, our feet pointed inwards, Black Tom once again looking like a cat rather than his true self.

I don't even remember having fallen unconscious.

The eldritch things of the island were gone; it was an empty land-mass.

The island was shaking.

IV. Voyage From the Unknown

We all arose the very moment we awoke, signalled by the bloody and limping Black Tom to follow, and spared no time in doing so. The ground beneath us shook and crumbled as we ran after the still ever-so-swift but crippled feline, our downhill descent enhancing our speed. In reaching the lifeboat, we didn't need to push it out to sea as the beaches had already sunk; it was drifting away and we had to swim for it, the cat jumping and awkwardly balancing upon my back; he shared with true cats that aquaphobic behaviour.

Climbing aboard the lifeboat, we heard a choir of whale-esque clicks, whistles, and pulses, before two were suddenly dragged under just as they were lifting themselves up, and blood bubbled to where they had once been. Black Tom hissed; we had nothing to fight them off with. We stood on the lifeboat in a circle, all facing outwards, prepared for a fight we held no advantage in.

One of these mermaids sprang up suddenly and grabbed me by the throat with its one hand, preparing its chela of the other arm to decapitate me; but Hayes intervened, allowing his arm to be broken by the chela instead of my throat, and wrestled the fish-woman into the waters, where he would be dragged farther and farther down by her, wrestling in that mixture of red, blue and black until out of sight.

The boat was toppled, and we had to now face the mermaids in the water, giving them the advantage. I saw the mermaids approaching, baring their teeth, when suddenly, a shark emerged, biting the tail in its entirety from one of the mermaids, leaving her to struggle as she bled to death. The remaining two mermaids showed genuine surprise before they took to assault the shark, grabbing to the piece of netting still upon her from when I had cut her out of it.

One mermaid lost her hand when letting it too close to the jaws, and in her panic, and now without grip upon the shark's net, allowed herself to be decapitated; the final mermaid sliced open the shark's belly with her great chela, but lost grip on the net, too. As the shark's blood and organs emptied into the ocean, she was able to turn and make one final attack, removing a chunk from the mermaid's torso so large the shoulders connected to the tail only by some remaining thin strings of flesh. The shark stopped swimming, and was gracefully lowered into the depths, a trail of red following after her to her final resting ground; the mermaid cadavers floated sickly to the surface.

We swam back to the lifeboat, and managed to flip it back over, helping one another to get in. Seven remained.

We were guided by Black Tom, raising our shirts and lying awkwardly during rests to cover ourselves wholly from the sun in our journey; the cat seemed unbothered by by the sun's rays. He took care to keep us from drinking the salt water of the ocean as we grew thirsty, scratching lightly at our hands if we tried to reach in. It was during this return voyage Samuel, whom I had never really acquainted with in spite of us both from the British Museum, even both having gone to the same university, suddenly became less quiet and talked on end all his knowledge of marine life; he noted, for instance, the great white that saved us from those mermaids must have been a female, not only due to her size being rare for males, but also the lack of claspers. It was interesting to hear him go on; a much need distraction from the island, so we did not return our bodies but leave behind our minds. Even Black Tom would sit and listen to his speeches.

The cat's scars and cripplement gradually faded over those two days, healing fully to his former self by the time we were spotted by a freighter, which we were rescued by and, in thanks to, were able to return to our respective homes; but you know all about that.

Black Tom insisted on being hidden as we were brought up, running off from me as I put him down the first moment I could find no one, save those from the sunken Emma, would see. Him running off was the last I saw of him in this tale, and none other saw him on that freighter either; he had returned to lurking within the very same shadows he had emerged from for all I knew.

THE THING WITHIN

Then fear left, and wonder, awe, compassion, and reverence succeeded in its place, for the sounds uttered by the stricken figure that lay stretched out on the limestone had told us the awesome truth.

HPL: The Beast in the Cave

Cast your judgement unto me, and throw me in whatever cell as you see fit, but I will not sway from the truth and deny my innocence from what you accuse me for your sakes.

As I have said, my friend had been acting strange for many weeks, going outside of his house less and less, refusing to let anyone see him; even his communications through other means gradually died off, until his very existence had seemingly ceased to be. Many of us tried to check in on him, but what few times he answered he would tell us from behind a closed door to head back from whence we came. This exercise of going to his house and knocking to receive no welcome became a standard routine of my life, until one day, the very same day I would be brought in for a crime not mine, the front door had been left open. Now, as is proper, I did not simply enter his house, but knocked on the opened door repeatedly, calling several times out to him, yet again receiving an answer of silence. And so, I headed in, fearing his gravely injured, or dead, but what I found was a fate much more horrifying than either.

As I took my steps farther into the house, the air immediately felt different, the internal structure of the very building seemed somehow weaker, and I myself grew shorter of breath and more miserable with every step. My way was marked out by droplets of dried blood, heading up the stairs, where spores suddenly appeared and grew thicker as I drew closer to my true destination. At first I did not see it through the fog of spores, but upon the ladder leading to the attic, there lay, what I did not realise until I had picked up and subsequently dropped it in fright, a skin, the full skin, of my dear friend, separated from the rest of him, blood marking tears torn from within. I perhaps should have ran, perhaps I may have, if my attention was not caught suddenly by a weeping from the attic. And so I climbed up, dreading who—or what—the weeper may be.

As I entered, the atmosphere of the attic became more spore than air, and the weeping grew quiet. 'Leave me, Joshua,' he said in an oh so familiar voice. When asked who he was, how he knew my name, he only cried again for me to leave. There was a torch by my hand. I picked it up. I turned it on, and, with shaking hand, steered the light to the weeper, dropping it the very moment I saw the weeper in full. A disgraceful sight it was, man-like in shape, but serpentine in its true nature, save for any tail, with gill-like holes all down its chest, opening and closing in breaths to puff out those dreadful spores. I could not move, paralysed in fear and misery, and so the weeper began to speak again, more clearly but with no less depressive defeat in his voice:

'Hitherto have I thought myself a dweller of the Earth, until my false-skin sagged away, the positioning of my face around the eyes moving out of place so to reveal it was always just a mask; I tried all I could to keep it on, to hide the hideous truth, to keep this grotesque monstrosity hidden away, but to no avail.' What had become of my dear friend paused, until I had picked up the torch again, so I could look upon his scaly face; 'what am I?' he said at last, black tears streaming down from either eye; 'all I know of myself is that I am afraid.'

I said nothing, I only fell down, as the spores invaded that attic and purged it of oxygen. In my next moments, I had awoke outside the house as it was burning, finally able to breath again, covered in his blood from when his injured self must have carried me out.

And so ended the suffering of his reality.

HERMES

Once more came the voice of my friend, still hoarse with fear, and now apparently tinged with despair:

"I can't tell you, Carter! It's too utterly beyond thought—I dare not tell you—no man could know it and live—Great God! I never dreamed of THIS!"

HPL: The Statement of Randolph Carter

There he was, each time I came into the pub known as Sheehan's, hunching over the table, with none other joining his lonesome booth, slowly but surely fulfilling an apparent mission to drain New England of all its alcoholic contents; there he would be whenever I entered, there he would be still as I left, always with a glass in his hand, one that would never be empty, as if the bar was his one and only true home, a place he had been born and would also surely die.

On one evening, I had found myself wandering over to his booth, pushed forth by a queer craving to know what this man knew—I knew he knew a great deal, a great deal what should never be told, a great deal what would better be left to die with he who carried such forbidden knowledge, but, like a fool, I was drawn to the bacterial symbionts (the mere fact he held otherworldly information) of what made this otherwise uninteresting fish glow like a star in the intellect-void space alcoholic establishments are known to be.

I took my seat opposite him, and while no words were exchanged, a conversation had passed between the two of us facially. 'I know what you seek, and no, you do not want it,' his sleepless eyes seemed to say; 'but I do,' responded I in face alone; 'no,' his eyes continued, pink from sleep deprivation, 'such great horrors must not be spread.' This silent talking of faces continued to and fro, wearying our facial muscles and eyes over what seemed to last for untold aeons, until he had finally broken it with the voice of mouth: 'very well,' he said with no emotion.

The withered man used what little strength of his body sleep deprivation and alcoholism had yet to take away from him to raise his glass and down what all of what content remained, closed his eyes, and, just for the briefest of moments, shivered, not in coldness, but in genuine fright of his own thoughts. Then his eyes opened suddenly, his glass was refilled with one of the herd of bottles that sat upon the table, and he began with an introduction: 'I used to be a man of academia—a man of mathematics and astrophysics, but now,' emotion faded into his words, and that was shame, 'now I can barely count, and the date, even to the month, is a mystery to me. And that is a good thing, I must keep my mind buried below the poison of ethanol, lest it thinks and remembers the shape.' His eyes locked with mine, and he continued: 'I know what your question is, "why would a man destroy his own mind?" And it is quite a simple one to answer; I force the decaying of my mind because the knowledge I hold is one I must not remember in full; if I remember, I know I cannot understand—no man can—what it is I know, and it will destroy my mind moreso than any drink could. Little by little, if I destroy that cancer that is thought from my mind, it may be gone, and only then will I be free from the great unknown that plagues me with fear.'

He stared at his newly refilled glass, hesitant to continue, but I was a patient man and could wait ...

'I used to work for the space agency,' he finally began, 'that is how it came into being—this tale, that is, of the nightmare that lurks in the heavens; I do not know its origins; we will speak of that ... that *thing* when we get there.'

He quickly took a sip of his drink, and paused with a sigh.

'So long as the task is simple, you don't need to send a man to space, an ape will suffice; in this instance, we had trained a chimpanzee, and given him his namesake from the Greek god Hermes—do not bother to look for any pictures or data on this chimp and this operation, all records have been destroyed, and what survives lives only between my ears, I can assure you of that—, which we had given to him as Hermes was god of travel, and what greater travel is there than that of the great black sea of space?' The astronomer smirked at this line as if it were the saying of a fool, drunk what was left of his drink, and refilled his glass. I had only drunk sips of my own, still on the first glassful, but he topped it up all the same, his eyes insisting I should be as much of a drunkard as he if I wished to continue listening, and continued; 'of course, Hermes was also the god of language, and what Hermes—the chimp, that is, not the god—saw up there that day was beyond the language of any mortal creature to describe, and any creature what cannot be granted description is one beyond conception; that is to say, it is an impossibility.

'We had sent him up with a camera to take images of the cosmos, but he only took one—one image of what shattered his mind the very moment he looked upon it.'

He paused with a shudder, palms pressed momentarily to his eyes, as his mind unwillingly tried to force together a puzzle of uncountable non-Euclidean pieces, but no two pieces would fit; it is clear now that his mind had only survived so long as it had been able to tell itself a lie, that the pieces only refused to fit together because he did not have a complete collection of all the pieces; but even with each and every piece, the puzzle could never be pieced together by a mind as simple as Man's.

'When Hermes came back down,' he eventually continued in great discomfort, 'he was frightened stiff. You could move an arm up and it would simply stay there; he was alive, but he wasn't ... there; a body with no mind to guide it. Later on, as all was being swept under the rug, he was euthanised, and his body cremated, his ashes scattered unceremoniously, any evidence of his existence destroyed and denied. But before then, we had to take a look at that photo ... that one photo taken at the exact moment the mind of Hermes died.'

The astronomer hunched over onto the table, hands on his scalp, fingers crooked at such an angle the nails that scraped his scalp lay almost flatly against it; his hands slowly scraped his scalp and twisted to slide the palms across his face, until he had four fingers covering each closed eye

(see not the unknown),

his thumbs pressed lobule over tragus to plug the canals

(hear not the unknown),

and his palms kept his mouth caged

(speak not the unknown);

a strange, low rhythm of struggle came from the cords of his throat, and slowly his hands uncovered his mouth

(it mustn't be spoken)

to reveal clenched teeth, his ears

(it mustn't be heard)

red and pale, and his eyes

(it mustn't be seen)

which had grown days more tired and bloodshot, newly added markings over the eyelids from his nails.

'I saw it,' he said suddenly but quietly. 'Not it all, otherwise my mind would have gone the way the mind of Hermes did, but I saw enough of it, I remember now.' He reached for one of his bottles lazily without looking, without looking towards anything at all, knocking it to the floor where it smashed; his eyes still fixed on to the abyss of his broken mind, he grabbed a shard and began carving in to the flesh of his arm to give a pallette of blood, and with the fingers of his uncut arm drew upon the table what he had seen. I should have stopped him, but my mind was transfixed on this reality-based rendering of a creature from the unreality, and with every detail I grew evermore faint and dizzy as my mind attempted to calculate how something what cannot be can, in fact, be.

'This is what I saw—or as close as I can show you, and I am glad I was not the one to bring this photo out,' the astronomer's voice had grown to one hysterical and been taken between quick, sharp breaths, 'no, no. I heard screaming as it was being produced, yes ... the screams of a man who was split, split in two, his body here in reality, but his mind sent elsewhere, but the ties between mind and body were somehow unsevered unlike that of Hermes—perhaps Man is ever so slightly more resilient than a chimp's, but still are we truly weak—, and when we came rushing in, his hands had clawed out his own eyes and thrown them to a fire he had started in that very room, and he continued to dig farther and farther into his face, perhaps in some attempt to destroy the brain, to end the madness-induced suffering; but as the other tried to keep his hands from clawing his life away from him, I looked into the fire and saw for what purpose it was started, not for his eyes (although it is likely true that he, in his madness, thought destroying the organs that give sight would, in turn, destroy the mental image of what they had showed him, though this unfortunately did not do any such thing, and he was locked in a padded room with his armed tightly bound for the rest of his days, until he bit off his own tongue and choked on it), but for the camera and the photo it had taken—I saw the slightly burned image of impossibility.'

The astronomer remained silent for some moments, his arm dripping blood to the floor, until eventually he stood, without uttering any words, and for the first time, I saw him leave the stool, as others grew pale in horror watching a trail of red form as he went, and leave the pub; I was still transfixed on to the blood image, but I managed reach a hand over to smear it, so no other mortal soul would see what I had seen, the great impossible thing.

That night was almost sleepless for me, and, too, have all since then been; for such an unreal being to exist within the realm of the real should not possible be, and yet it is so; it is not possible for me to put down in words what should not be, so I can only describe the effects it has to see even a glimpse of such a thing: my mind is too overworked trying to make sense of what cannot make sense to sleep, but I do still sleep whenever my mind fades away too fatigued to continue its aeternal attempt to finish an endless, senseless, incomplete puzzle, yet this work will continue slowly in my dreams as they are plagued by the horrors of the implications of such a thing to be; I find myself bursting into fits of hysterical laughter, or weeping a mad hyena, when my mind does on some occasion think it has connected two pieces (which, of course, it cannot), and there have been times I have been told of doing such things, even rambling nonsense as I did so, but in which I have forgotten—it is, I believe, in these instances, my mind does force a connection between two puzzle pieces, but cannot cope with such a connection, and so enforces memory loss as a defence-mechanism to save my sanity.

I tried to find the astronomer to ask of him how he coped with such horrors plaguing his mind, for I had taken to the drink just as he did, to help me forget, but to no avail. Unfortunately, my only hope was gone; I eventually tracked him down to find he had taken his life the very night he told me of all, the night he remembered what the drink had made him forget; walking into his home, his arm still bleeding, had hanged himself, but not before painting the walls red with blood to say: *IT CANNOT BE, IT DIES WITH ME.*

His final note is one of confusion, because, unless this thing truly is something which can only survive if people know it exists (which I do not believe to be the case, as Hermes had discovered it, and it must surely have existed before he laid his eyes upon it for it to have eyes laid upon it), there is no reason to conclude killing oneself would kill the thing. However, there is another explanation: both instances of *it* refer to differing matters; the first *it* is what Hermes discovered, and it is indeed an impossibility, thus *it cannot be*; the second *it* refers to the knowledge of knowing such a thing exists, for if no one living knows such impossible beings are up there, then no one can be told of them, plaguing their minds with such horrors, as mine has become, thus *it dies with me.*

It is thus I know what must be done, to cure my mind of the horrors, and to keep the horrors of knowing the unknowable from spreading, I must end my life. I have a razor to the side of where I sit now, on my bed, and I prepare to slit my wrists, and repeat the astronomer's message as I do so, in case of its importance being needed again.

I have a bottle of the same alcoholic beverage the astronomer always drank—as this choice of beverage only felt right—to have as my last, to loosen my nerves for what I must do, both in a sense of not being halted by human's innate fear of death, and, if I am fortunate, for my last moments to be of less agony than they would otherwise be.

THRONEIS

It all began, old Ammi said, with the meteorite.

HPL: The Colour out of Space

OCTAVIUS ANGLICUS

In the isolated village Throneis, known to no maps, few have entered and fewer have left for all its history; populated always by no fewer than fifty, and no more than one-hundred-and-fifty; though, if one were to walk through it during daylight hours, one may assume it to have been deserted by its inhabitants centuries ago, with the natives too afraid of the Sun to ever leave their homes, which have seen so little upkeeping, overgrown with moss and mould and flowers and grass, and some even trees, with many collapsed walls and roofs to be seen; one would expect glass to litter the ground from shattered windows, but no windows have ever been built.

In the night they gather, without need of torches to light their path, for they have the eyes of cats, and gather to the central house all others encircle in spiralling fashion, the only with a second floor and basement, the only upkept just enough so as to not collapse, nor to be engulfed by the forest, as the others have been, where the thing awaits their coming.

Slumbering in the basement of dust and webs in the day, the Thing slithers up to the attic in the night, to look spaceward whence It came crashing down centuries ago, where It yearns to return. The natives interrupt Its melancholic longing for the ritual It commands of them.

All the ever-impregnated woman-natives kneel one by one, the Thing slithering endless slimy limbs within each female subject to inspect every crevice of her sex; the welfare of Its parasitic kin within their wombs must be raised with great care, while allowing enough room within the very same wombs for the natives to continue breeding their own kind, for they are the incubators of a far greater being, a superior organism from the depths of the Great Black Sea Above. This parasitic reproduction cycle has continued to mutate the natives more with every generation, their faces becoming flatter and squaroid, the facial features shrinking so as to appear a giant holds the features of a man, their nails removed entirely and their digits lengthening to resemble suckerless tentacles more so than fingers and toes, their hairs growing out as tumours of miscellaneous flesh and teeth, their torsos comically smaller than their limbs and heads; there will come a generation where all recognisably human elements will no longer be found at all; they will be Its true kin, greater than the tumorous slug-things the incubators have been birthing for Its consumption.

The thing that the natives had for centuries before worshipped will be their first consumption, before ejecting themselves into space, and shattering their own forms to countless spores finer than the finest grain of sand which will spread across all galaxies across all realities, each never landing until a host is found. The spores can always detect a host.

And that is where the cycle begins once again, and continues in aeternum.

VOID

Naught is there for Man,
In the Great Black Sea Above,
Horrors beyond the known,
Give to his mind a shove,

He will cry out in fear,
With naught found to belove him,
Only the great devourer,
Who beholds many a great limb,

It lurks in the void,
Stay clear of the void.

CLOSE

The end is near. I hear a noise at the door, as of some immense slippery body lumbering against it. It shall not find me.

HPL: Dagon

Nigh on naught is there what causes such a great fear of the unknown to arise within me than the ajar door what I am certain had not been open before; always is it that I find a door left open, in spite of my growing obsession to close any and all doors I pass through, or, on the most dire of occassions, will I see the door open ever so slightly before my eyes, creaking with every sudden nudge it recieves from the other side. Never have I found someone—something—within my home when a door was ajar, nor was anyone—anything—on the other side of an ajar door—not even those opened before me—on those few occassions I could gather myself the will to check. Yet, when I leave the door ajar, and only observe, there is always an oddity which multiplies my ever-growing fright: a shadow of some monstrous shape lurking in my eye's corner, dancing through the gaps betwixt door and door-frame, scurrying itself away as I look toward it; a creaking floorboard of someone's—something's—weight pressing down against it; that daemoniac breathing so faint I am uncertain of its existence outside my mind.

Never do I truly believe the lurking daemon to be gone, to not always be ever so close; no creaks of floorboads, nor any other sounds of movement, are ever made to show it moving away from the door, yet it is gone all the same each and every time I open the door and check the other side.

And what always succeeds in keeping me uneased as I find myself afore an open door is knowing that the intruder is just as much within reach of the door as I am: if it is able to open the door and I close it, then we both are surely as close to the door as the other is.

THAT WHAT LIES BELOW

I fear this monstrous lurker of the other side of the door, even though a logical analysis should conclude it is not there, that I simply have a habit of giving myself a fright over a strangely common occurence of doors opening all by themselves, because I simply know that it is indeed real, even if it be a creature of the unreal; and one day when I open a door, the monster will not pass from sight into hiding, but remain there for me to see, and do unto me its bidding.